STEVEN JOHNSON AND THE MISSION 2

YASHESH RATHOD

Contents

CHAPTER ONE

A DEAL GONE BAD

Johnson and his partner walked on the street flanked by residential buildings. The Bio-attack on the city Johnson was in Hong Kong had taken place forty-eight hours ago. The air looked clear enough but there might be residual effects lingering in the air, and that was why he and his partner, Chris, wore gas masks. The whole city had been quarantined and the street was completely empty. Both men had parachuted from a jet and had landed in the middle of the city.

Through the gas mask, the muffled voice of Chris came, 'Look at this all carnage. Who could've done this? Why?'

'That's why we're here, Chris. Intel suggests that we will find our answers at an apartment which is marked on our GPS,' came the muffled answer from Johnson.

'What's there? What are we gonna find there?' Chris asked.

'According to the intel, a brilliant scientist named Dr Serizawa had been secretly working on a powerful bio-weapon in a small lab in his apartment. If we search through his apartment, we might find a clue to trace it back to the people to whom he might've sold the weapon. Remember the tape that has gone viral about terrorists ready to attack more cities in China until there is nothing left in it? Unless they are given what they want, that is trillions of dollars of money from the federation, the attacks will continue and move on to another country,' Johnson explained.

When Johnson and Chris reached the locked front door of the building in which Dr Serizawa had his apartment, Johnson ordered his partner to set the charges on the locked door. Chris did as he had been ordered and blasted the door from its hinges. They entered the building and climbed up the stairs until they reached the eighth floor. Johnson ordered Chris to hack the security panel beside the door. So, Chris brought out a hacking tool, hooked it to the panel, and began hacking.

After a minute, the door unlocked with a beeping sound. Johnson and Chris entered the living room and without wasting any time began rummaging through things. Upon finding nothing they moved on to the kitchen and then to the living room.

'Admiral, take a look at this,' said Chris, staring at a book on the bookshelf.

Johnson walked to Chris, and Chris showed him the book he was interested in amongst other books. 'Sir, if you look closely then you will see that this wooden object is painted to look like a book. Plus, I can't pull the book out of the shelf either,' explained Chris.

'Well, let me see,' Johnson said and observed it for a moment. He moved the book sideways but it would not budge. He tried to pull it out of the shelf but he failed there too. Lastly, when he pushed it inside, the book, like some kind of button, went in. A moment later, a secret door opened in the wall. Both men entered the secret doorway and found themselves in a pitch-black room. Chris and Johnson brought out their torchlights and started observing the room.

The room was the secret lab in which Dr Serizawa must have done his experiments for making the bio-weapon. In the light cast by the torch, Johnson found a diary lying on a desk amongst a mess of beakers and flasks, and he opened it to find what it was.

While Johnson was going through the diary, Chris was rummaging through things around in the lab. In the diary, Johnson found nothing but a series of chemical formulas and other experiment related notes, until he got to the page where he described having a meeting at the local cathedral for the purpose of selling his bioweapon to somebody called Lucian.

'Hey, Chris,' Johnson called over his shoulder.

'You, found something, admiral?' Chris asked.

'How far the local church is from here?' Johnson asked.

'Let me see in my digital map, sir,' Chris said and after concerning the map for a moment he said, 'It would be an hour of walk from here, sir. But why?'

'This diary I'm holding is of Dr Serizawa,' Johnson said by holding the diary up for Chris to see. 'This diary says of a meeting where Dr Serizawa must have sold his bio-weapon. We just need to get there and see the footage of CCTV cameras planted in the cathedral.

Chris nodded thoughtfully.

When they were about to leave the apartment, a hellish sound came. It was like some wild, rabid animal. Both men just froze on the spot in the lab. Nobody spoke for a minute until Chris saw something enter the lab and uttered, 'Oh my god! What is that?!'

By then Johnson had got his sight on that too. It was Dr Serizawa but there was something off about him. He knew that the head was of Serizawa but the body he had was not of his. It had resembled a giant black spider walking on its eight legs. Chris, frightened, instinctively pulled the pistol he had holstered from his thigh and aimed at the creature.

'Stop there, Dr Serizawa,' Johnson called to the creature. But seeing that the creature had no effect on it, Chris pulled the trigger and put a bullet into Dr Serizawa's head before the leapt creature landed on one of them. The creature was in the air when Chris had fired, crashing the creature at their feet and spilling the blood on their boots. The creature squirmed on its back for a moment before going silent.

Leaving the dead Dr Serizawa behind, both men exited the dark, secret lab and the apartment. They were still in the apartment building climbing down the stairs when they saw, on the landing, a woman banging her head on the blood-red spot of the wall constantly.

'Mam, stop that. You're gonna seriously hurt yourself,' Chris called to the woman.

The woman stopped banging her head and slowly turned her head towards Chris and Johnson, who stood on the stairs. As soon as the face had turned, the horror was revealed to both men. At several parts, the face of the woman had been fleshless as though a rat had gnawed it out, and bones could be visible. Because of no flesh to cover the lips, there had been a grim smile, ear to ear. The eyes were the most horrific feature. They were bloodred and luminous.

The woman, stretching her both hands forward, started to walk menacingly toward Chris and Johnson, who in panic took a few steps back up the stairs.

Chris once again pulled the pistol and fired a shot. The shot was missed purposefully and the bullet was buried in the wall. Chris had wanted to just warn the woman, not shoot her. But the woman didn't deviate from her sight in the slightest from both men.

When the woman was an inches away from Chris, who had his gun trained on the woman and was shouting nervously for her to stay back, he heard a bullet flypast beside his left ear. Chris jerked his head right and looked back to see a smoking gun held by Johnson.

Chris returned his attention to the woman who had been pushed back by the impact of the bullet but resumed to move toward Chris with her hands outstretched. A few more bullets were fired, sending the woman backpedalling to the wall. Seeing the woman groggy, Johnson pushed Chris aside and ran to the woman. He did a powerful roundhouse kick to her head and silenced the woman.

'What the hell was that, admiral?' Chris asked, trying to wipe the perspiration off his forehead but his hand was blocked by the full face glass of the mask.

'They are mindless killing machines, The B.O.W. - the product of Dr Serizawa's bioweapon,' Johnson explained. 'No matter what happens, never take off your mask until we're out of this city.'

'Aye, admiral. Wouldn't want to be turned into one of them,' said Chris.

When Johnson pushed the door open of the apartment building, he saw no movement on the street so they decided to take a walk to the cathedral until something better came up.

They walked and walked the street until they reached a parked car. Chris broke the window of the car with the butt of the gun. As soon as the window broke, the car gave out a loud siren. The siren would bleat for another five minutes. Chris tried to hardwire the car but found that it was out of gas. Luckily the gas station was just up ahead. But the car being out of gas was not the only problem they faced. From every direction those B.O.Ws began walking towards them, slowly closing them in all directions.

Johnson and Chris stood there in the cacophony of the siren. After a minute the Siren went still and all they could hear now was the horrific growls of those B.O.Ws as they, with their outstretched hands, came nearer by second.

'We can't push the car all the way to the gas station,' Johnson continued, 'We need to fill the gas in a container and empty it in the tank of this car while fighting against these fiends. It is our only way. Are you ready, kid?'

Chris nodded nervously.

'Reload and move fast to the gas station,' Johnson said and they fired their way among the B.O.Ws to the gas station.

Both men were back to back. Johnson was moving towards the gas station while Chris back peddled and covered the admiral's six. Johnson took three steps and stopped. He fired a few shots, clearing his way to the gas station while Chris took care of his back to keep the B.O.Ws from attacking from the back. He then took a few more steps. Every now and then when one had to reload, they called out a loud warning "Reload!" and the other one covered his partner while he was reloading. The cycle of moving, stopping, firing and reloading continued until they were in the gas station.

In the gas station, they found a container. Johnson filled it up with the gas from a pump. 'I won't be able to fire as this heavy load will use up both of my hands,' Johnson said while lifting the red can of gas. 'You've gotta cover for me while I carry this to the car.'

'Aye, admiral. Just follow me while I clear the way,' Chris said.

Ten minutes had passed and Johnson was pouring the content of the container into the tank of the car. Meanwhile, Chris made sure that no B.O.Ws attacked Johnson and of course, him. Chris was constantly firing the B.O.Ws left and right, front and back to survive.

'Done!' came the voice of Johnson as he closed the lid of the tank. 'Get in the car! Get in the car!' Johnson shouted while grabbing his gun and adding his shots to those of Chris. Both men opened the door while battling against the B.O.Ws. In a few moments, Chris hardwired the car and the car roared to life. All three of the windows were being assailed by the B.O.Ws. One of them actually was able to grab the neck of Chris through the driver side window that had been broken by Chris earlier. Johnson trained his gun on the B.O.W and called to Chris to lie back on the seat.

Chris did as the admiral told him and that gave Johnson a clear view to shoot at the B.O.W. Johnson fired six shots until his gun made clicking sounds suggesting that it had run out of bullets. The grip by now by the B.O.W. had loosened on Chris, so he put the car in the first gear and floored the accelerator. In front, the B.O.Ws were thrown off as the car hit them. Some were run over. The one that had grabbed Chris hung by the window of the moving car until Chris grabbed the gun with one hand and put a bullet in the B.O.W's head.

'Phew...! That was a close one, admiral,' Chris said.

'What is your ammo status?' Johnson asked.

'Three more magazines,' Chris answered.

'I'm dry. Used the last magazine to save you from that B.O.W. from the window,' Johnson said. 'How far is the local ammunition shop?' Johnson asked.

Chris concerned his digital map while keeping his one eye on the road. 'It is half an hour of drive from here,' Chris answered.

'Set a new waypoint to there. We might as well restock our ammo if we want to stand a chance against more B.O.Ws we might encounter in our way,' Johnson said. 'Keep those headlights deem; We don't want to attract more B.O.Ws.

*

Johnson and Chris were in the ammunition shop strapping themselves with combat knives, ammunition belts, grenades and pipebombs. The shop didn't have the federation's high tech weapons like plasma or laser guns. But it did have a good choice of rudimentary firearms. Johnson chose the M16A2 assault rifle while Chris liked to keep the Spas-12 shotgun. Both men had decided to carry their pistols too for any quick reflex combat situation.

As soon as they were ready to leave, a bullet entered the shop and buried itself in the floor inches away from Johnson's boots. They had been standing in front of the wooden counter which they jumped behind to take cover.

Next, the barrage of bullets began to bury themselves in the wooden counter, pinning both men on the spot. When, after a minute, the barrage stopped, Johnson chanced to look up the surface of the counter. He saw nothing. Johnson knew that the attackers had not left yet, but only waiting for them to come out in the clearing. He gave a sign for Chris to retreat to the backdoor. They opened the backdoor and entered the dirty backyard. A man with a machete was waiting for them. As soon as the man saw Chris and Johnson, he, with his luminous red eyes, darted to them, swinging his machete violently.

It was Johnson who got attacked by the man first. But the blow of the machete was parried by Johnson with his assault rifle. He kicked hard in its gut, sending the B.O.W.

flying back. Johnson ran to it and foot-stomped the B.O.W's head so hard that like a watermelon it squashed.

They climbed a ladder that led them to the terrace of the nearby building. When they were on the top of the building they had a clear view of the attackers hiding behind the parapet wall of the opposite building of the ammunition shop. Johnson fired the first bullet, sinking it into the forehead of a B.O.W hiding behind the parapet wall of the building, and that began the firefight that lasted for fifteen minutes. In the end, Johnson and Chris took out six of the B.O.Ws. After that, they climbed down the ladder, entered the ammunition shop from the backdoor and exited the shop. They looked around before entering the car and driving away.

*

(Three days ago)

'I'm gonna be late...oh I'm gonna be late,' Dr Serizawa muttered to himself while he scurried around in his secret lab as he made a sample for his finished bioweapon project. He stirred the blue liquid in the beaker and when he was satisfied, poured it into a small flask. He then grabbed a suitcase and placed the flask in it carefully.

He exited the door of his secret lab and went to the toaster to grab the toasts he had put in for the breakfast. Holding the buttered toast in his mouth and the suitcase in his armpit, he locked the door of his apartment and climbed down the stairs. He bowed to a woman and two men in his way as a way of saying good morning.

It was 9:30 A.M. and he was headed for a meeting in the cathedral with a possible customer of his product.

When he had reached in his car to the church, he had butterflies in his stomach. The meeting was going to be held in a private room of the cathedral with a man called Lucian

Lee. Dr Serizawa entered the cathedral and went straight for the secret room. Inside, he observed there were a few worshippers on the benches. The secret room was in the far corner on left. On the door to the room stood a guard clad in a white suit.

'We've been expecting you. The boss is in the room already,' said the man in the white suit and stepped aside to let Serizawa enter.

'Aaah...Dr Serizawa! I've been waiting for you. Please take a seat,' Lucian Lee invited.

Serizawa nodded with a forced smile and sat himself down on a chair at the round table facing his host.

There were four men - each in a corner. There hung a beautiful chandelier from the ceiling that filled the room with its vivid light. The floor was carpeted and the walls had beautiful tapestries hanging.

'So, Dr Serizawa, how's everything?' Lee asked to break the ice.

Serizawa observed that Lee was a tall man with Chinese facial features. He had a robotic left eye and a robotic left hand. He had a bassy voice. Lee looked to be in his fifties. He wore a green sleeveless shirt and white pants.

'Fine!' Serizawa answered shortly.

'Man of few words, you are, Dr Serizawa, I see,' Lee said.

Serizawa said nothing but smiled.

'So, let me get to the point of the meeting then. Have you brought it, the product of my interest?'

Serizawa lifted the suitcase and opened it, showing its content to Lee, which is a small flask holding a powerful bioweapon the world had ever seen. He snapped closed the suitcase and put it on his lap. 'It is powerful stuff. One small dose can decimate an entire city. And it is also my life's hard work. The price better be right for it otherwise I will not sell it to you,' Serizawa said.

'You will get whatever money you want. Just tell me what it is? Lee asked.

'I want three million in exchange for this,' Serizawa lifted the suitcase a bit from his lap before putting it back.

'Done!' Lee simply said.

'You agree?!' Serizawa was completely caught off guard by his client's answer. He had never thought that he would be able to sell it at that price. He had purposefully put the big price so the haggle would bring it down at somewhat fifty thousand or something. He knew his product was worth more than that but he was broke and needed money desperately, so, he jumped up with the answer "Yes!".

'Your account will get credited with three million tomorrow,' Lee acknowledged Serizawa.

'Oh. Sure, sure,' Serizawa said excitedly while bowing to his customer. 'I believe, this belongs to you now,' Serizawa said while handing the suitcase to Lee. 'I give you the most lethal bioweapon - The Hadakva virus. Based on the blood type of the host this virus acts differently. You will find some infected which I like to call B.O.W. to be more intellectual than others. You will find some infected obtuse while others smart to solve complex problems and communicate with each other. You could even give them weapons and they would combat like gorilla warriors. Some B.O.Ws you will find more powerful than others, having the ability to shapeshift into a lethal weapon of destruction.

'My B.O.Ws will be harder to kill, stronger to defeat and smarter to challenge. With them, you could win any fight or war,' Serizawa said.

'That's good. I'm delighted that you've created a destructive wonder, Dr Serizawa,' said Lee.

*

It was payday and it was already past the pay-time and he was getting nervous with the thought that he might have been cheated. The afternoon turned into evening and evening into the night but he found no increase in his bank balance. It was midnight when he woke up to drink some cold water from the fridge to beat the summer heat and the growing worries about his money. When on the way he looked out the window, he saw a dot coming down from the sky. For a moment he stood there trying to figure out what it was. When the dot came nearer the object became clearer and he saw that it was a missile heading for the city. He ran and hid under a sturdy table. He felt a ground shake once, suggesting that the missile had hit. Next, he heard the glass of the windows break. The green fog began entering his apartment. Serizawa coughed and choked heavily and his body began to shapeshift into something hideous. Dr Serizawa was no more, and his place had been taken by a monster. He had become the first of the B.O.Ws.

CHAPTER TWO

B.O.Ws

Chris and Johnson were in the moving car when they heard a roar of an animal. Chris pressed the brakes and brought the car to a screeching halt. They were at a square and Johnson looked in all four directions to find the source of the sound. No sooner had Chris opened the door than an elephant broke through the gate of a zoo that was a few paces away from the car. The gate made a loud clanging sound as it landed on the road. The elephant looked berserk and twice the size, due to the effects of the virus, of course. It was a B.O.W. The elephant quickly set its sight on the car and started to move toward it.

'Go!go!go!' Johnson shouted.

Chris got back in the car and floored the accelerator. The Mammoth-like elephant almost crushed the car with its feet. But that was not the end of it. In the mirrored rearview Chris saw the elephant giving a chase. Johnson couldn't believe what he was seeing. He knew that elephants are good at running but 90 km/s?! In fact, the elephant was gaining on them.

'How could this be possible, admiral? An elephant running to match our car's speed?!' Chris shouted behind the mask and under the roar of the car's engine.

'The virus affected the animals as well. We're not dealing with a natural animal but a B.O.W.' shouted Johnson.

The car went almost 120 km/s and the infected elephant matched the speed.

'We can't shake it off our trail like that going in a straight line. We need to go for the evade manoeuvre,' Johnson shouted.

'Understood!' Chris shouted back.

The ground shook slightly as the huge elephant chased the car. Chris then pulled the handbrake and turned right sharply and started to turn left and right haphazardly. He did that for fifteen minutes but it was without success. They couldn't shake the B.O.W. off their trail. Then Johnson moved to the back seat and with the butt of his assault rifle broke the rear glass of the car. He then started shooting at the chasing B.O.W. He aimed at its legs, head, and body and it slowed it a bit. Taking advantage of that Chris put some distance between the car and the B.O.W.

After five minutes, they had their car parked in the gap between two buildings. They were seated in the car silently when they saw the elephant walk past them. It would be foolish to go in a car as the sound of the engine would give away their position. So they decided to abandon the car and climb down a manhole that was just behind. They entered a sewer.

'Chris, set a new waypoint to the cathedral,' Johnson ordered.

'On it, sir' replied Chris.

After a moment, they were heading in the direction of a subway.

*

(At the federation's HQ)

Mike Morrison was sending the recording between Johnson and the HQ to Lutsi, the terrorist base. Once finished, he got to the bathroom and made a call to Lucian Lee, the head of Lutsi.

'Sir, I've sent the recording. Seems like two men named Admiral Steven Johnson and Chris Watson are headed to the Maji Cathedral to get the CCTV footage of the meeting between you and Dr Serizawa. You will find more details in the recording,' said Morrison.

'Well done, Morrison. Your loyalty will be rewarded. I will see to it that those men don't get to their destination. Keep me posted with the updates. Your cooperation is very important to me,' Lucian Lee said and hung the phone.

Morrison got out of the bathroom walked to his seat and settled once again at his terminal of the Federation.

*

(At the Lutsi HQ)

Leo Anderson entered a building after punching a security code into the wall panel. The door swished open and he walked to the out-of-order elevator. He gave his retinal scan and the elevator opened. Anderson pressed the big red button labelled with "Do not press!" and the lift began its descent below the ground. It took three minutes before the door reopened, revealing a tunnel-like passageway. The passageway was well illuminated with artificial lights. Anderson walked until the passageway turned left and he entered a giant multi-floored room with hundreds of people working. There were glass staircases connecting the floors.

'Hey, Lucy. How's the boss's mood today?' Anderson said after walking to the workstation of a woman.

'He has an assignment for you,' Lucy said.

'Da! That's why I'm here,' Anderson said.

'How about a dinner at the restaurant after the assignment?' Anderson asked.

'We will see,' Lucy said and both of them flirted with each other for the next few minutes until a phone rang. Lucy picked the intercom. 'Can I get you something, sir?' asked Lucy.

'Is Anderson here yet?' asked Lee.

'He is here, sir' Lucy said.

'Then, send that killer right to my office,' Lee said and hung up the phone.

Lucy looked at Anderson and nodded. Anderson understood what it meant and started walking to the office of Lucian Lee on the third floor. No sooner had Anderson taken a few paces than Lucy called out from behind. Anderson looked back to see Lucy give him the flying kiss. Johnson made a gesture of catching it in the mid-air and putting it inside his shirt. After a quick wink, Johnson turned and resumed walking to the boss's office.

*

Lucian Lee was seated behind a desk on a comfortable chair, smoking a fine cigar and sipping red wine from a glass. He had been in an argument with his man in charge of the setting up of the meeting with Serizawa, demanding reasons for the foolishness of not taking care of the surveillance cameras of the cathedral before the meeting.

Knock...Knock came the sound from behind the door when he was deep in his thoughts. Lee saw on the big-screen monitor that it was Anderson at the door. 'Come in,' Lee spoke into a small mic. The door opened and Anderson walked into a luxurious room, which was the office of Lee.

'Have a seat, Anderson' Lee invited.

Anderson accepted by setting himself down on a couch in front of Lee's desk. 'Loved what you've done with your office, boss,' Anderson said while looking around in the office.

'It's been a while Mr Anderson since you last completed my assignment,' Lee said.

'Almost a year, boss since I put bullets to the high profile men in Bagdad,' Anderson replied.

'I hope that a year of doing nothing hasn't rusted your skills,' Lee said.

'Nah. I've been doing a lot. I have opened a small movie theatre and I am learning to play the Harmonium. And there are other things I have been doing to improve my skills,' Anderson said.

'I was talking about your skills to kill people,' Lee said with a heavy tone.

'Oh, I'm still sharp as a blade when it comes to killing people,' Anderson said with a grim smile.

'Good, because I have more killing for you,' Lee continued, 'You see, I set up a meeting with our client at Maji cathedral. The cameras there were forgotten by my staff and the whole meeting lay recorded in the database of the cathedral. Two men are on their way to collect the footage and they will send it to the Federation's HQ. If that happened my identity will be revealed and the existence of Lutsi will be as good as over,' Lee continued after sipping wine from the glass, 'Are you catching my drift, son?'

'You want me to kill those men and destroy the footage?' Anderson asked.

'Excellent! Where can I get more guys like you?'

*

Anderson was in the armoury of the Lutsi's base, gearing up for the mission. He had been offered a few men as a backup but he had refused by saying that he was a lone wolf and liked to work alone. His plan was to get to the cathedral first and ambush the two men before destroying the footage.

Once he had geared under the casual clothes, he walked to the garage and turned the key in the Kawasaki motorcycle. The engine roared into life and he rode out of the huge trapdoor-like gate which opened into the ground. He then set the GPS to the destination city which had been attacked with Hadakva virus and speedily headed to it.

*

Johnson and Chris were navigating through the sewers when they saw a shadow of something. As soon as Johnson was going to discard the shadow of a small rat, a giant B.O.W rat scurried around the corner. Both men began firing as the rat lurched to them. It took a whole magazine of the assault rifle to kill the enormous infected rat. Both men then resumed their path to the cathedral.

After half hour of walking in the sewer, they came to a blockade. It was vines blocking their way. Chris was gonna move closer when Johnson placed a hand on his shoulder, stopping him abruptly.

'What is it, admiral?' Chris asked.

'These are no ordinary vines. The virus has affected vegetation as well. See those thorny things there?' Johnson pointed to tentacle-looking things in the vines. He then picked an empty can of beans from the trash down on the ground and threw it toward the vines. As soon as the empty can landed near the vines, two tentacles grabbed it and screwed it as if it was a piece of paper.

'Woh...' Chris reacted. 'That would've been me if you hadn't warned me, admiral.' Chris said. 'Think a grenade can take care of it?' Chris asked.

'No. The whole ceiling will come down on us if we use a grenade down here,' Johnson suggested.

'So, what are we gonna do, admiral, to get past this?' Chris asked.

Johnson then brought up his pistol and aimed at the tip of a tentacle. When the bullet hit the tip, the vines retaliated with an attack of their own. From the tips of both tentacles were shot something which knocked the pistol off Johnson's hand with a powerful blow. Both men understood immediately to evade it or get killed.

At the end of an interval of three seconds, the tentacles shot something, which Johnson and Chris tried hard to evade by doing all kinds of diving while shooting back. This evading the attacks and shooting back continued for five minutes before the two of the tentacles died down.

Chris stood up and saw that Johnson had already reached the vines, cutting them with the combat knife.

On the way onwards they fought more B.O.W rats and deadly vines with tentacles.

*

It had been three hours Anderson had been riding his motorcycle at 130 km/s on an open road. He stopped at the blockade of cars of local police lining the border of the city.

'Sir, you can't go in there,' a police officer said to Anderson.

Anderson showed him the forged badge of a high ranking officer of the Federation with his photo on it.

The police officer observed the badge and saluted Anderson, handing him the badge back. 'Sir, the virus has spread to the whole city.'

'I know. I'm here to investigate within the city,' Anderson said.

'Sir, you will have to put on a mask with a breather. We have one for you here,' the officer called, 'Hey, Parker get me the breather kit.'

Anderson shook his hand as if to say no. 'I've brought one,' Anderson said and put on his helmet back before pressing a button from inside of it. The helmet transformed into a high tech mask covering his whole face. 'Now, officer if you'll be kind enough to make a way for me to pass the barricade?' Anderson asked.

'Oh, yeah. I forgot. The officer made a sign to other officers and a car was driven out of the line to make a way for Anderson's motorcycle to enter the city.

Anderson grabbed the clutch, hit the first gear and rode through the gap in the barricade and headed towards the city under the moonless night.

*

When Anderson saw a horde of B.O.Ws lumbering about on the road, he shot a small missile from his high-tech motorcycle. The missile exploded on hit on B.O.Ws, sending the infected up in the air and clearing a path for him.

The path to the Cathedral passed the city zoo on the way. Anderson had no idea that a beast was loose in that area. But when he heard the loud roar of something he understood that something was not right here. The ground started to shake suggesting that the problem was nearing him.

Anderson glimpsed in the rear-view mirror to find a giant elephant chasing him at incredibly high speed. Johnson fired a missile from the rear part of his bike. The missile hit the B.O.W. but didn't seem to have done more than a scratch. Anderson twisted the accelerator to full but the B.O.W matched the speed. There was no way Anderson was going to outrun it. It seemed that the beast would chase him to the end of the world.

When Anderson was going to give up, an idea came to his mind. There was a self-destruct mechanism built into the bike he was riding on. If he somehow used that firepower properly, the beast could be destroyed. All he had to do was voice-command the bike and in the same instant, the bike would detonate with an explosion that would level even a building.

Anderson put the bike on auto-pilot by flipping a switch on the dashboard. He then, with his one free hand opened a secret compartment of the bike and pulled out a bag-pack. He put it on and in the next moment, the thrusters came out of the backpack suggesting that it was a jet pack. Anderson stood up on the bike, balancing his weight on it, and jumped up in the air. The powerful thrusters flung him up in the air like a bullet from a rail gun.

When Anderson was out of the blast radius, in the air he voice-commanded in his wristwatch for the bike to self-destruct. No sooner he had commanded the bike than a bright light blinded Anderson followed by a deafening sound of the blast. Anderson hovered in the air until the light was gone and he saw no trace of B.O.W. that had been chasing him moments ago. He saw no sign of his motorcycle either. Both, the motorcycle and the beast, had been blasted to small pieces.

*

The jet pack ran out of fuel and Anderson was forced to land on the roof of an outdoor rock-concert stage. He climbed down a maintenance ladder to the stage and made his way to the front of the stage. He saw a couple of B.O.Ws lumbering about in front. He brought out a black box from his pocket and put his finger on a scanner on it. The red light captured the fingerprint and authenticated it with a beeping sound. Then followed a series of transformations of the box that turned it into a plasma sniper rifle. It was a nano-technology at its best. He brought out another box and did the same and the second box turned into a plasma pistol.

Anderson shot one of the B.O.Ws lumbering in front of the stage, but that was a mistake because it attracted more of them. Anderson then was engaged in popping heads of the incoming B.O.Ws with his plasma rifle.

A few minutes had passed and the infected kept coming, trying to corner the stage from all directions except the back of the stage which was a closed structure. Now, the infected started to climb up the stage and reach for Anderson. Anderson had to find a way to keep the B.O.Ws off the stage.

After popping the heads of countless infected, he found that a pyro technique was available for the stage and he turned it on that covered all three of the directions which made a wall of spark and lit all the infected that walked through it. The pyro lasted for a minute and in that time majority of the B.O.Ws were burned. Seeing an opportunity to escape before more of them arrive, he jumped off the stage and made a run for the exit while turning back occasionally and popping more heads with his excellent marksmanship.

Anderson had walked for some time after exiting the concert stage perimeter when he encountered a new threat. A deformed B.O.W. had been lying on the road which just sat up when Anderson got near. The B.O.W. got to its feet and picked up something from the road. It was a chainsaw that it must have been using for work before he was infected. He pulled a string of the chainsaw and turned it on. The machine gave a roar as the B.O.W. started swinging it wildly.

Anderson took a shot with his plasma pistol on its head and fired. The head of B.O.W. jerked back a little but nothing more happened, in fact, that shot to the head had made it angry. Menacingly it darted to Anderson. Anderson continued firing shot after shot till it reached for him. Upon reaching proximity, Anderson dodged its chainsaw attack and got behind it. He then back paddled while shooting constantly, his target being its head. A dead B.O.W. body on the road made him fall and he landed on his back. Before he could get up, the chainsaw attack came upon him. At the last moment, he rolled out and kicked up to a standing position. He fired a few more shots and back paddled again, the B.O.W. with the chainsaw turning to him and chasing back to decapitate his head.

When again in proximity, Anderson pulled his assault rifle from his back and blocked the chainsaw attack. The B.O.W. continued to press the roaring chainsaw down Anderson's throat while Anderson pushed with his all might the assault rifle that was blocking the chainsaw. The Chainsaw lowered and went up and lowered again on Anderson. At last, Anderson broke the struggle by kicking the B.O.W. in the gut following it with a point-blank shot from his plasma assault rifle. The B.O.W. got groggy from the damage. Grabbing that opportunity, Anderson snatched the chainsaw from it and gave a powerful swing at its head. The head of the B.O.W. was cleaved clean from its shoulders and fell on the road. A jet of blood burst out of the neck of B.O.W. and after a moment the body crashed onto the road too. Anderson switched the chainsaw off and threw it aside before continuing his way to the cathedral.

CHAPTER THREE

THE CATHEDRAL

In the sewer, Johnson and Chris climbed a straight ladder to the ceiling. When they were under the lid of a manhole, they heard funky music and the sound of machinery that was muffled due to the lid. Chris lifted and pushed the lid aside and climbed out. Johnson waited for Chris's signal.

'All is clear, sir. No B.O.Ws here,' Chris called from above over the music that was loud now.

Johnson climbed to the surface and found himself in the middle of a live carnival. All the rides with colourful bright lights were empty but were running for some ghostly tourists. Recorded audio announced something in Chinese on loudspeakers there were everywhere throughout the huge area of land upon which the carnival had been built.

'Sir, we're here,' Chris said while pointing to a map of the carnival on a stand. 'and we need to move that way in order to get to the exit, sir.'

As soon as Johnson nodded he saw a horde of B.O.Ws led by six of the huge sized clowns sprinting towards them. Chris followed Johnson's gaze and he saw that too.

'To that roller coaster track! Hurry!' Johnson ordered and both men ran like their lives depended on it.

Both men reached the coaster and climbed to the coaster's track, the horde of B.O.Ws chasing behind. The carts were not on so both men carefully traversed a meter wide track. The track was at a much altitude so they tried not to fall.

B.O.Ws got on the track too and started sprinting carelessly which led to some of them slipping and falling off the track. Johnson traversing behind Chris, from time to time, looked behind and shot at the B.O.Ws to slow them down. Just one bullet was enough for each B.O.W to make it lose its balance and fall, except for the huge clowns that were resilient and refused to go down, but luckily, unlike other B.O.Ws, they chose to walk down the track rather than sprinting.

Johnson and Chris had reached halfway of the whole circuit and they observed that B.O.Ws were traversing from the other side of the track too. Soon, they will get surrounded and it would be their end.

Both men stood back to back, firing at the nearing B.O.Ws from both sides of the track. Just before the B.O.Ws gained on both men, Johnson shoved Chris off the track before jumping off the track himself.

Both men bounced off the smooth fabric of the giant tent that was beneath the track. They rolled down the tent and to the ground. They didn't waste any time catching their breaths but headed for the exit.

*

It had been an hour and both men were spinning in a vertical merry-go-round wheel, trying to figure out a way to get out of the situation they were in right now. Johnson and Chris had been surrounded by B.O.Ws an hour ago and the wheel was the last solution they had resorted to.

When the cart reached the maximum altitude, both men looked down at the thousands of B.O.Ws that surrounded the wheel. The boarding platform was thronged so there was no way for any of the men to get off the wheel. The cart was kind of open but due to the fast-moving wheel, none of the B.O.Ws was able to touch them.

Then a suicidal idea came into Johnson's mind and he discussed it with Chris.

'Sure it will work, sir?' Chris showed his doubts.

'It is either that or be stuck spinning in this wheel for eternity while those monsters are in wait down there,' Johnson said.

'Understood, sir,' Chris agreed to his plan and made a cross sign as if to pray the God.

Johnson began his plan by grabbing a grenade from his equipment belt. He steadied his breath and pulled the ring. He waited for a second before tossing it at the centre of the merry-go-round wheel. The explosion took place as soon as the frag grenade made contact with the centre, dismantling the joints and freeing the wheel. Both men braced themselves as the wheel started traversing on the ground. Luckily, the carts were strong and didn't get crushed under the weight of the whole wheel.

The wheel crushed every B.O.W in its path and leaving a trail of blood behind, headed for the north wall of the carnival while both men screamed madly from inside the cart, their whole world spinning.

There was a collision between the wheel and the two-storied administrative building of the carnival and the wheel was stopped. It stood still vertically as if frozen in time for a moment before crashing to its side. By the time the wheel crashed, their cart was on the bottom part of the wheel so they evaded the worst of the crash but that didn't mean that Johnson and Chris weren't hurt. Both men struggled out of the cart with their broken bodies and limped away from the wheel. Chris had gone out cold from the crash and it was the slaps from Johnson that had brought his consciousness back.

The administrative building, which was adjacent to the perimeter's tall wall, was levelled from the collision with the wheel and that had broken a portion of the perimeter wall and made a gap in it. Both men now wouldn't have to go for the exit gate to escape this carnival of terror.

Through the debris of the levelled administrative building, Johnson and Chirs limped and made their way through the gap in the perimeter wall and out of the damned carnival.

*

Under the strong moonlight, Anderson arrived at a jetty and looked for a decent boat to steal. With his motorcycle destroyed, Anderson had chosen to travel on the water to get to the cathedral faster since the streets would be filled with hordes of B.O.Ws that would only slow him down. But he didn't know the danger that lurked in the water.

Anderson chose a small boat docked in the water and unmoored it. It took him a minute to unlock the engine's lock with a pin. Once the engine roared to life, he manned the boat and drove away to the opposite bank that lay lined with silhouettes of buildings in the far distance.

When the boat reached some distance from the jetty, Anderson felt a jolt as if the boat had hit something. He dismissed it and continued to drive the boat. All of a sudden there came another jolt that almost tossed Anderson off the boat. Anderson stopped the boat and looked around for a clue of what had been hitting, the boat bobbing madly on the water surface. A few seconds later a giant shark emerged partially on the surface and hit the boat strongly, throwing Aderson off into the water. All of his weapons were thrown off in the process and sank down the water.

Anderson knew that sharks didn't grow that huge and decided that this one had been mutated due to the virus. He was up against a marine life B.O.W. The B.O.W. shark emerged from the distance and swam towards Anderson who was swimming his way to the boat, his limbs splashing in the water madly.

It was close when Anderson got on the boat and the shark swam past under. It was a fishing boat so it had a harpoon gun attached to it. He found plenty of harpoons lying together in the boat. Anderson grabbed one and loaded it into the gun. The shark had rounded back in the distance and with its fin only visible, swam towards the boat. Anderson waited for the right moment to shoot and focused his aim.

The shark was ten meters of distance from the boat when it emerged on the surface and opened its jaws wide as if to swallow the whole boat. Anderson aimed into the jaws and let go of the harpoon. As soon as the harpoon hit inside the jaws, the shark went under the water again and swam past under the boat. The water slowly became red suggesting that the shark had been hurt. But Anderson knew that it would take more than one harpoon hit to take out the beast.

By the time the shark rounded back, Anderson had loaded the gun with another harpoon and was aiming now. Using the same strategy three times he hit the shark two more times.

Anderson was bent to pick a harpoon from the boat's deck when the shark changed its tactics and hit the boat throwing Anderson off into the water again. Holding the harpoon still, Anderson pressed a button in his belt and his body was covered in an energy shield.

He was swimming back to the boat when his left leg was grabbed by the deadly jaws and he was dragged under the water. Anderson struggled to break free but it was to no avail. He remembered the harpoon still in his hands and thrust it down the eyes and brains of the beast. It was a series of six thrusts before the grip on his leg loosened and through the blurry vision deep in the water and by the light of the hundreds of phosphorescent small fishes that swam in the surrounding, Anderson saw the B.O.W. sinking with its belly up. He let go of the harpoon he was holding and swam to the surface.

After getting on the fishing boat, Anderson checked his energy shield which had been reduced down to only two percentages. If it was not for the shield, his left leg had been mangled and lost. He turned the energy shield off. It was now useless until it was recharged again at the Lutsi headquarters. He sat on the deck of the boat for some time and tried to catch his breath before moving further on his mission. He had a change in plans. Due to the loss of his all weapons, he was not gonna bother killing Johnson and Chris at the cathedral as he had decided to, instead, he would just grab the footage of Lee's meeting with Serizawa and purge the whole system of data.

However, he had one final weapon. Two seeds of a plant that he would use to kill Johnson and Chris. The seeds were given to him by Lucian Lee. It was engineered with the virus. All he would need to do was to plant it in the ground and add some water. Just in fifteen minutes, the seeds would start to grow into carnivorous monster plants.

*

Johnson and Chris had been fighting a giant plant, its huge and lethal vines making a ring-shaped perimeter boundary of the cathedral. There was no way past those vines. Chris had tried to destroy a portion of it with the lob of a grenade. But as soon as the vines were destroyed, new ones took their place. The only way past was to destroy the twenty meters tall two B.O.W. venus flytrap plants.

Johnson and Chris were dodging the toxic acid the mouths of the plants spat at them. The plants were bulletproof but Johnson had found weak spots in the plants and advised his partner to aim for those. Both men did their best to dodge the acid spits while shooting with their pistols at the weak points that looked like mushrooms in the mouths of the plants.

When the plant took enough damage, its both mouths crashed on the ground, jaws wide open as if crying out in pain. Within ten seconds both mouths rose again and resumed their acid spits.

'Shoot at the weak points,' Johnson yelled while dodging the acid attacks.

'Sir, It's got no effect,' Chris replied.

'Trust me. I've got a plan,' Johnson yelled while shooting at the mouths of the plant.

It had been a minute of dodging the acid spits and shooting at the mushrooms that were inside of the plant's mouths, and finally, both mouths again swayed for a moment and crashed on the ground. Johnson saw that and ran to one of the mouths, pulled the ring from a grenade from his belt and threw it inside the plant's mouth. As soon as the grenade got in, the plant's mouth closed tight as if to have caught a fly.

Johnson had moved to a safe distance when an explosion inside blew the mouth to bits. By this time the second plant had risen and was back to throwing spits of acid. Now that the plan was clear to Chris, he and Johnson were back again weakening the plant so that they can get an opportunity to blow the plant from inside.

But when the opportunity presented and a grenade was thrown into the mouth by Chris, it was spat out and the grenade exploded outside. The plant was clever and a new tactic was needed to take it out.

'Fall back ... fall back,' Johnson yelled while dodging the acid spits and both men back paddled while shooting and got behind the cover of a building. Suddenly, Johnson's eyes fell upon a huge drilling vehicle parked nearby and an idea formed in his head.

Johnson sat on the passenger seat while Chris tried to hardwire the driller. When the engine roared to life, Johnson got on the driver seat and drove the vehicle through the one-storied building that was between them and the B.O.W. plant. After he had decimated the building, Johnson honked the vehicle's horn to get the plant's attention and with the drill spinning noisily, the plant was torn to shreds.

With the plants dead the perimeter fence of vines died down instantly making the cathedral accessible from all directions. Johnson parked the driller outside the cathedral door and both men entered the holy building.

When they reached the surveillance room, Chris sat immediately at a terminal cracking the authorization to access the system files. It took him five minutes to achieve that but he had bad news after rummaging through the system.

'Sir, the system has been purged clean of all data. The system log says the purge took place an hour ago,' Chris said from behind the mask.

'Damn!' Johnson smashed his fist on the wooden table he was standing at. 'Someone got here before us. We've lost our only chance of finding out who's behind the Bio attack.'

Just when Johnson was beginning to lose hope for the mission, the comm crackled.

'Federation to Chris and Johnson. I repeat Federation to Chris and Johnson. Do you copy?' came the voice from the comms.

'This is Steven Johnson.'

'Sir, we've got an update on your mission. You're required to get to the LZ as soon as possible. The chopper will be waiting for you to bring you and your partner back to the HQ. We've caught a mole in the HQ that may give us information on the terrorist group. You're required at HQ to interrogate the mole named Mike Morrison. Over.'

'I'm on my way. Send me the coordinates of the LZ. Over.'

*

Johnson and Chris had ridden their way on the drilling vehicle to a hospital building upon which a chopper would be waiting. On the way, they had run over countless B.O.Ws on the streets. They were now climbing countless stairs of the tall hospital building.

'Who the hell ... puts an LZ over ... seventy-five flights of goddammed stairs,' Chris complained, his body panting heavily from the exhaustion of climbing.

'HQ said ... rest of the streets were hot with B.O.Ws ... so they chose the tallest building in the area ... where it would be safe to land away ... from the threat from any of the B.O.Ws.' Johnson explained while panting.

When the door was opened to the terrace, both men witnessed something they were not expecting. Instead of an empty terrace with a chopper sitting in the middle, the whole place was hot with B.O.Ws. The chopper was there nonetheless, but it hovered up in the sky, trying to find a way to land.

'Sir, I can't risk landing with these many of B.O.Ws down there,' the pilot's voice crackled in the comm.

'Give us some time to clear the LZ,' Johnson replied in the lip mic.

There were about hundreds of B.O.Ws covering the large open area of the terrace and without wasting any time both men began clearing the place with their weapons.

Over time the number of B.O.Ws kept on reducing until it reached about fifty when a hellish scream was heard. Seconds later that scream came again. In the distance, Chris saw a creature jumping from one terrace to another. It was making its way to the terrace they were on. Chris was busy fighting the remaining B.O.Ws so he didn't give it much attention and that became his grave mistake. From down the creature, all of a sudden, jumped high in the air and clung to the chopper. It then leapt downwards and landed on Chris. Johnson had no idea what was going on, and neither did Chris. It happened very fast.

It was when Johnson turned to Chris' lying body on the terrace floor, a creature sitting on Chris' chest, eating the flesh of his stomach, Johnson knew that he had lost his partner. In the rage, Johnson emptied the whole magazine of his assault rifle on the creature and killed it. He then cleared the terrace of the remaining B.O.Ws.

Johnson ran to the still body of his partner and bent down to check any vital signs despite there being a wide hole in his stomach. But there was nothing he could do now. He took Chris' mask off and put it on the floor beside him. The body had been infected by that agile creature so Johnson couldn't take it to the HQ for a proper burial. He closed his eyes and made a cross sigh across his heart. After a few seconds, he stood up and saluted the dead body, tears pricking behind his eyes. When he was done giving the tribute to his partner, he turned to see that the chopper had landed.

CHAPTER FOUR

CHAOTIC STREETS

Mike Morrison sat on a chair behind a desk in a room lit by a hanging lightbulb over the table. It was Federation's interrogation room with one wall of glass through which people observed the interrogation process from outside. At the opposite of the table sat Johnson ready to begin the interrogation process.

Johnson bent forward, his face entering from the dark to the light cast by the overhanging bulb. 'Mike Morrison...' Johnson started 'if it is your real name. We checked your phone and found that you've been sharing a lot of confidential information with this "Boss" named contact of yours.'

Morrison did nothing but stare into the eyes of his interrogator.

'Your recent share of information cost me my latest mission and my partner. Since I'm no gentleman, I will ask you nicely once after that it will be the hard way,' Johnson said and waited for his words to sink in the mind of Morrison before continuing 'So, Who is this "Boss" and how for long have you been working for him?'

'I will tell you nothing. I would rather die than reveal the identity of my boss,' was the firm reply from Morrison.

'Oh. So you're one of those loyal types. Man, I hate those. It makes me do things I hate the most, that is employing nasty interrogating tactics,' Johnson said.

'Try out your best but my loyalty will remain intact to my boss,' the mole said confidently.

Johnson smiled and said, 'We will see about that.' He pushed his chair a little back and sat on it with his feet on the table. With his hands upon his head and feet crossed on the table, he seemed like in thought. 'There are hundreds of ways to spill someone's beans and I am deciding the least painful one for you.'

By now, Morrison was perspiring a little from the thought of what he might face.

After a minute, Johnson swung his leg off the table and stood up. 'I've got a perfect solution for you. I saw it in a movie once,' Johnson said and exited the interrogation room.

*

It had been an hour since Morrison was hung upside down from the ceiling of the interrogation room alone with a rope. The room's door opened and Morrison saw in his inverted world Johnson enter the interrogation room.

'So, an hour of upside hanging has changed your mind?' Johnson asked.

'Not telling you anything,' Morrison replied, his body swinging lightly as he fruitlessly tried to break free of his bounds.

'Thought so, that's why I've brought this pet of mine,' Johnson said while lifting a small cage he was holding for Morrison to observe. 'They say this species of rodent is excellent at gnawing anything.'

'What are you gonna do?' Morrison asked, a horror crossing his face.

'Sure, you want to tell me nothing?' Johnson asked for the last time.

Morrison gulped in fear and replied hesitantly, 'No.'

Johnson clicked his tongue as if disappointed and put down the small cage with the rodent in it. He brought out a bag of white cloth from his pocket and bent down beside the cage. He opened the cage and connected the opening of the bag with the opening of the cage. The rodent scurried into the bag. Johnson then raised the bag to Morrison and inserted Morrison's reluctant head into the bag and tied it around the neck.

As soon as Johnson sat on a chair to watch the show, the rodent began gnawing at the parts of Morrison's face. The whole upside-down body of Morrison twisted in pain madly and Johnson poured beer into the glass and started sipping from it, watching his interrogation technique at work.

With every passing minute, the cloth of the bag became more bloody as the rodent was munching on its victim's face. After five minutes, Johnson walked out of the room and returned after a minute with a bowl of peanuts in his hand. He sat on the chair and began enjoying the nuts.

It was after fifteen minutes when Morrison's cry of pain turned to submission saying, 'I will talk. I will talk. I will talk ...'

Johnson put the bowl of nuts on the table and leisurely untied the strings of the bag from around the neck. In a minute he had the rodent back into its cage.

The face of Morrison was bloody and hard to look at. Blood dripped on the floor from his face. 'I will tell you whatever you want to know,' said Morrison with the panic of what he had just gone through.

'Let's start with this "Boss". Who is he?' Johnson asked.

'He is the head of an organization called Lutsi. His name is Lucian Lee and he has Lutsi headquarters built up underground under a tall Flash building in district 17 of Hongkong,' Morrison replied.

'Flash?! It is one of the leading DTH companies,' Johnson said surprisingly.

'Yes. And Lutsi owns it and runs its operations hiding behind the covers of it,' Morrison said.

The interrogation continued afterwards for about thirty minutes acquiring very confidential information on Lutsi.

*

Officer Chan helped fill the fifth bus with a number of citizens before he closed the door of it and slapped the side of the bus thrice signalling the bus driver to take them away from the city called District 17. The next empty bus stopped and the doors opened before him. Chan shot his pistol in the air to control the crowd of citizens that were eager to get aboard the bus and leave the city.

It had been three days since Mike Morrison revealed the head of a terrorist group to Johnson, and it had been two days since the desperate head of Lutsi announced a bio-attack in district 17. The people of the city were now being escorted out by the police to save them from the virus.

There was real panic on the streets. Shops were being looted, banks were being robbed and there was complete chaos. Good people were leaving the city while bad people were staying behind to uplift the hell.

The Bio-attack would take place in approximately thirty hours according to the last TV footage from Lutsi.

Officer Chan saw a black fancy car speeding its way to him in the distance. When the car stopped on the other side of the road, Chan gave charge of crowd control to one of his subordinates and went across the road to check.

Chan observed that the car was very weird and looked made for combat. The window glass rolled down and he saw a man in the driver's seat. The man showed his badge of the federation to Chan. Chan saluted Johnson and said, 'Sir, what can I do for you?'

'Give me the briefing of the situation here in the city,' said Johnson.

'Sir, the bio-attack is imminent and the whole city is being emptied. Troops of Lutsi have taken control of the streets with tanks. In addition to the bio-attack, there are bombs being placed across the whole city by Lutsi. It is chaos out there in the streets of the city. Thugs and criminals have remained behind to do whatever they want to. Choppers of Lutsi are patrolling the sky and destroying any resistance that is being put up by the military. It is hell here, sir,' said officer Chan.

'Thanks for the information, officer, I will see what I can do,' said Johnson and the window glass rolled up and the car accelerated with the roar towards the heart of the city. Chan scratched his head, trying to figure out how one man can fight an army. Shaking his head in disbelief, Chan returned to his former task on the other side of the road.

*

Johnson saw a glowing red on the ground beside the road and he pulled over the car. He got out and walked to the glowing red. It was one of the bombs officer Chan had talked about. It looked like a manhole lid half-buried in the ground. Johnson turned on the camera in his cap and linked the comm to the federation headquarters.

'This is Johnson,' said Johnson in his lip mic.

'We read you, Johnson. What do you want?' came the reply

'Connect me to the bomb disposal department. I've got a weird-looking bomb that needs to be taken out,' spoke Johnson in the mic.

'Give me a sec. I will get you to Janica, one of the experts in the bomb-defusing department.'

After a few seconds of static noise on the comm, a feminine voice came, 'Hey, Johnson, Janica's here. What have you got?'

'I'm bending over a metallic, round-shaped, glowing bomb as you can see in the camera,' spoke Johnson.

After a few seconds, the reply came, 'This is of a new technology called titan. This type of bomb has a digital core. Open up that panel on the left side of the bomb.' instructed Jenica.

'Are you sure I should touch it?' Johnson showed his concern.

'Don't worry, It won't blow up. We'd had these bombs in design for two and a half years before we made its prototype six months ago. The core is all digital and that means it can be hacked. Just follow my instruction and you will have that bomb sorted out in no time.'

Johnson did as Jenica had instructed and opened up the panel after taking out the screws of it. Inside was the mess of wires and different coloured jacks. 'Now, which coloured wire you wish me to cut?' asked Johnson.

'Nah, no need for that. Instead, move the wires carefully to reveal a yellow coloured jack hidden underneath them' Jenica instructed as the footage cast by Johnson continued to appear on her computer screen.

Johnson just did that and uncovered the yellow coloured jack. 'Now, what?'

'Grab the remote hacking tool's transmitter and hook it in the jack and I will do the rest from here,' she said.

Johnson pulled out a dongle from his pocket and inserted it into the yellow coloured jack. As soon as he walked to his parked car he heard the roar of multiple heavy engines. He got into the car and saw from his car's cameras that he was being surrounded by heavy tanks from all directions. He started the engine and pushed a button on the dashboard, bringing the car's energy armour online.

An enemy tank fired a barrage of bullets followed by a missile from another tank. Johnson saw the status of the car's armour depleting fast on the monitor and pressed another button on the dashboard. As soon as the button was pressed, the car began to transform.

While the assault continued, the car kept on transforming until it became a kind of tank itself. Johnson then let go of the wheel and opened a compartment in the car. A Joystick controller lay there which Johnson grabbed and began controlling the tank of his own like some sort of video game.

There were nine tanks in total that surrounded Johnson. He used the side thrusters of his car tank to dodge the incoming missiles. An enemy tank fired a locked-on missile and Johnson fired his car's machine gun to take the missile out before it could reach its target. The missile exploded with kaboom as the bullets from Johnson's car's machine gun hit the missile in the air. Johnson fired a missile from his car's Vulcan gun and took out an enemy tank that had no energy shield like Johnson's car. The remaining enemy tanks continued firing.

For the next fifteen minutes, Johnson did his best to use thrusters to dodge the incoming attacks, using the car's machine gun to take out locked on missiles and the Vulcan gun to take out the enemy tanks.

Once all nine tanks had been destroyed, Johnson faced a gigantic battle tank. Just one hit from it took out all of the shield's energy and another hit would surely destroy the car and its driver for sure. Johnson transformed the car to its normal state and drove away and broke the sight of the giant tank.

After he had hidden well in the distance behind a building, Johnson shot a small drone in the air and controlled it from his seat in the car. The drone was the size of a tennis ball which cast HD quality footage on Johnson's monitor. He observed the tank from the eyes of the drone and found that it was a type of tank called cobra. He searched in the Federation's database about it and after rummaging through it for a few minutes he found that this expensive type of tank was extremely powerful and hard to destroy. But there was one weakness. The armour in the small area in the back was non-existent. A cobra tank runs on some type of complex nuclear energy and from time to time it needs to discharge built-up excess energy from that part of the tank to avoid getting blasted. If that small energy ejection area of the tank in the back is hit with a perfectly aimed missile then the blast will reach the nuclear core, destroying the whole cobra tank with an explosion from inside.

Johnson's feed was cut as the drone was detected and taken out by the cobra tank. He then started the radar scan and found a moving red triangle some distance away suggesting that the cobra tank was still looking for Johnson and his car.

The battle had become a game of mouse and cat. Johnson was the mouse and he had to defeat an oversized and overpowered foe. He put the car on stealth mode and the car's engine became noiseless. Since the stealth mode put the car on battery power he couldn't speed the car past 15 Km/h.

As the centre dot in the radar neared the red triangle, Johnson's nervousness increased. One mistake and before he knew he and his car could be blown to bits.

The car was now hiding behind a building beyond which stood the cobra tank. Johnson waited and waited until the cobra turned its back to him. Instead, the cobra tank moved around the corner towards Johnson. Before it was too late Johnson put the car out of stealth mode and reversed the car and straightened it in one smooth motion. No sooner had the missile from the cobra tank been fired than Johnson floored the accelerator while activating the nitrous boost. The missile just missed its target and Johnson lived. Johnson sped the car so fast that the cobra tank couldn't keep up aiming its target and gave up.

Johnson waited for half an hour at the remote distance in the car before moving again in stealth mode towards the cobra tank that, like previously, guarded the bomb Johnson had examined. This time Johnson used a different building to hide behind. He had a plan this time. He fired a special missile that he had been saving for an emergency. He had fired the missile in the north in the air. The missile exploded with a loud boom and the whole night sky brightened. The tank moved towards the explosion and aimed at the sky, showing its back in the process. Johnson silently drove the car to a position where he could have clear shot to the cobra's back and locked a missile in the blue glowing round hole. Johnson pressed a button on the steering wheel and the missile was fired from the car. With an explosion from inside the cobra was destroyed before Johnson's eyes.

Johnson parked the car ten meters away from the bomb and got out. When he had walked to the bomb he observed that the device he had hooked into the bomb had a blinking green light.

Johnson turned on the comm that he had switched off before engaging in a battle with the enemy tanks. 'This is Johnson, over,' Johnson spoke in the lip mic.

'It's Jenica. Why your comm was offline?' asked Jenica.

'I had to deal with some intense threat and the disturbance from the comm could've cost me my life,' explained Johnson.

'Is the threat neutralized?' Jenica asked.

'Yes, It has been. Now, I have this blinking green light on the hacking device attached to the bomb,' said Johnson.

'I have finished uploading a virus to the bomb,' came the answer from Jenica.

'Does it mean the bomb's defused?' asked Johnson confusingly.

'No, but it can be now destroyed by blowing it up,' said Jenica.

'Blowing it up?' asked Johnson.

'Don't worry. The virus that I have just uploaded has decreased the blast to a birthday party's firecracker,' explained Jenica.

'Oh,' Johnson nodded 'How do I make it explode? Should I go for a random wire?'

'Never do that with a titan bomb. The cutting of wire would be considered a security breach in the bomb's core and the core will act by resetting the blast radius values to the maximum before blasting in your face,' Jenica explained.

'How do I detonate then?' asked Johnson.

'You need to supply a steady AC current until the core is overcharged and destroyed. Open up the car's bonnet. You will find a cable in it,' explained Jenica.

Johnson walked to the car, got in and drove it near the bomb before getting out and searching in the bonnet. He found a transparent cable of which the one end was lost somewhere deep into the mess of the engine. Johnson attached the other end of the cable into the jack Jenica instructed over the comm.

Johnson once again was on the driver's seat and turned on the engine. He pressed a glowing button with the letter C and the cable lit up bluishly as the current running through it became visible.

'Now use the accelerator to supply a steady AC current to the bomb's core,' Jenica instructed. 'Keep the pin of rpm meter pointed between 3 to 4, and that should be enough to overcharge the core.'

Johnson did as Jenica instructed and in a minute the bomb detonated with an explosion equivalent to a firecracker.

When Johnson had done detaching the cable and the remote hacking tool from the bomb and putting it back into the car's bonnet and his pocket respectively, four cars got past him chased by more police cars. Both sides were firing at each other wildly. Johnson got in the car and floored the accelerator. He was going to help local police to take down those runaway thugs in the cars.

Johnson reached behind the last of the police cars and craftily overtook it. In mere seconds he was ahead of all the police cars. The thugs continued to poke their heads out of the windows to fire bullets at Johnson. The thugs' cars were heavily armoured so Johnson had no choice but to use missiles in his car. One of the punks used up a rocket launcher and Johnson did everything in his skills to evade that. When the aim was locked onto a car, Johnson pressed a button and the missile did the rest. The car exploded and was thrown off the road like a toy car. Multiple rockets were fired by thugs and Johnson used the car's machine gun to take out those rockets before they hit the car. Some of the rockets managed to hit Johnson's car but it only took some portion of the car's energy shield. However, a few more rocket hits could take down the whole energy shield and make the car a bit vulnerable.

The chase continued across the city for about five minutes and now Johnson had shrunk the thug's crew down to one car. There were four thugs in the car and while the driver did every trick to evade, the men on the passenger seats continued to fling grenades, fire bullets and use rocket launchers at Johnson and the four police cars that were way behind, their engines unable to keep up with the hot pursuit.

One of the suicidal guys climbed out of the car's window and got to the top. Next, a big gun came up from the roof of the car. The gun was attached to an iron thick plate to shield the gunner. The thug brought the gun online and fired a shot at Johnson. It was a big laser gun and one shot from it completely took out the energy shield off Johnson's car. The next shot would blow it to bits. The laser gun was fired but this time Johnson was not in the bull's eye, instead, the shot was aimed at one of the police cars that had neared them. The police car stood no chance and was destroyed, killing the police terribly in it.

Johnson checked the scene in the rearview and cursed under his breath. He had used up all his missiles and he had to think of something else to take the thugs down.

He used the nitrous boost and aligned his car with that of the thugs. He then turned the wheel powerfully and rammed the thug's car so hard that it flipped several times before laying upside down. The thug operating the big laser gun from the car's roof had been thrown off like a ragdoll and lost, dead probably, and the remaining thugs climbed out of the turned car and made a run for it. Johnson let the police handle it.

*

Anderson had learned that Johnson and his supercar had breached all of the securities and were headed for his boss, that's why he sat in a cobra tank in the frontline with regular tanks surrounding the Flash building. There was no way for Johnson to breach this last defence put up by Anderson. Johnson would need a matching army of tanks to stand any chance or he could die trying.

As Anderson was giving instructions via the comms to his troops, he heard the rocket-fueled supercar roaring its way towards them. The car suddenly stopped at half a kilometre away and transformed into a tank, and from there started hurling missiles from its Vulcan gun which Johnson had restocked. Anderson wasted no time and ordered other tanks to attack.

There were around thirty tanks, not counting the cobra tank handled by Anderson. Johnson's car had no chance but he continued to give them the fight.

After fifteen minutes, Anderson joined the fray and with a press of a button took out the supercar. It was blown to bits and the same would have been the fate of the driver inside.

CHAPTER FIVE

HAPPILY MARRIED

Johnson saw from the top of a tall building as his remote-controlled car was destroyed. The controller he was holding started showing red light suggesting that the connection with the car had been lost. He dropped the controller on the floor after self-destructing it and brought out a grappling gun from under his belt. It was another of the fine gadgets provided to him by the Federation. The gun was powerful and could be used to travel from rooftop to rooftop. The building he was on was adjacent to the Flash building. He shot the hook of the grappling gun towards the lofty roof of Flash building. Just like he had travelled to the terrace of the building he was on, with the press of a button, the gun pulled him up swiftly and Johnson was on his way to the top of the Flash building.

The pull from the grappling gun was so great that Johnson was hurled up a few meters in the air above the terrace. After landing silently he saw that five snipers were posted on the rooftop. He would have to take them out before he could use the door that led down inside the building.

Johnson shot his grapnel to the small tower that was built on the rooftop of the Flash building. Silently he reached on top of it and had bird eyed view of the situation.

Three of the five snipers were patrolling the roof and only two were fixed to their spots aiming something in the distance. Johnson had no silent weapon. All he had was the handgun that would sure to make enough noise to give his position away.

Johnson observed the guards carefully while the backpack he was wearing began transforming into butterfly wings. It was a kind of glider and Johnson glided to the roof silently just behind a patrolling guard. As soon as Johnson landed behind the guard he grabbed the guard and elbowed him hard to his temple, knocking him out cold. Quickly, he furled the glider wings and grappled back to the top of the tower. He repeated the process of gliding behind a guard and taking him out until there remained only the two stationary targets. But then a radio crackled from one of the taken out guards, attracting the attention of a stationary guard.

The guard walked to the sound of the radio and found out what had happened. He quickly called the other guard and both of them began assessing the situation. A plan forged into Johnson's mind and he quickly threw a smoke bomb toward them. The cloud of smoke completely hid them and while putting on the special goggles Johnson glided into the smoke. In the thicket of smoke, guards were unable to see a thing but Johnson's special goggles outlined the guards with red colour, making the takedown easy.

*

Anderson was outside his cobra tank watching the supercar of Johnson burn when his radio crackled with a feminine voice. It was his sweetheart Lucy.

'Leo, you need to get in the building right away. An armed man has breached the securities of the Flash building and he is headed straight for the boss's room,' Lucy said.

'On my way, honey. That man will regret breaking into the headquarters,' Anderson said confidently and ran for Flash building's entrance.

When he reached supposed to be the out-of-order elevator that would take him down underground to the base of operations, he heard the sound of gunshots being fired and immediately took cover.

Moments later when he saw Johnson climbing down the stairs in the feed of cameras cast to his wrist monitor, Anderson looked as if he had just seen a ghost. But it was not time to wonder about things and he tried to ambush Johnson by hiding behind the wall of the elevator.

Anderson waited and waited for his target to get into the attacking range. Eventually, when Johnson walked to the elevator and stood there trying to figure out to open the elevator doors, like a tiger, Anderson leapt on him. Both men crashed to the floor and the gun from Johnson's hands got thrown.

Both men wrestled for a minute on the floor before Johnson brought a military knife from his belt and both men separated. Anderson pulled a combat knife of his own from his boots.

The first swing came from Anderson which caught Johnson's left cheek. It was a slight cut but the blood started to trickle from it. Next, Johnson made a swing and Anderson parried it with his own blade. Anderson swung the blade at Johnson's feet but Johnson avoided it by quickly jumping over it. Next came the thrust from Johnson and Anderson backflipped. The battle of knives continued between them for the next fifteen minutes until both men got exhausted and Anderson made a mistake, and as a result, Johnson plunged his blade into the chest of

Anderson.

Anderson dropped to his knees and started coughing blood on the floor. He then produced from his pocket an injection and he stabbed it into his neck, injecting the green looking substance into his system.

Moments later, Anderson pulled the knife from his chest and dropped it down, He was under transformation of some kind.

Before Johnson's eyes, the man changed into a B.O.W. He looked like a spooky ogre now with his left hand becoming a round shield of bone.

Johnson immediately leapt towards the gun in a corner and grabbed it while Anderson walked slowly and menacingly towards Johnson. Johnson fired a barrage of bullets from his handgun but the bullets were blocked by Anderson's shield-like left arm.

The ogre got in proximity and swung his right hand, which had turned into a talon with sharp blade-like nails, at Johnson. Johnson ducked and dived away from harm's way. Johnson had noticed that the part where his blade had buried deep in Anderson's chest had revealed his beating heart. He figured that if he attacked that vulnerable organ, he could kill the ogre, but the question was how? Every time he shot, the ogre blocked his bullets with his left shield arm. He would have to think of something.

The ogre continued to block Johnson's fired bullets and swung his taloned arm at Johnson, while Johnson ducked, dived, shot and ran for his life. It was after fifteen minutes that the ogre made the mistake of charging at Johnson at full pelt. Johnson dived away at the last moment and the ogre crashed into the wall hard before falling on his back and knocking itself out. Johnson took the opportunity and put a bullet into its heart which transformed the ogre back into Anderson. Anderson lay on his back, gasping for air while Johnson entered the elevator and went down to apprehend Lucian Lee. Slowly everything faded away by the eyes of Anderson and went black. He had been a good asset to Lutsi and now he was dying just like one of the expendables.

*

Anderson gained momentarily consciousness and found, painfully, himself looking at the bunch of doctors and Lucy, his girlfriend, moving him on a stretcher in the hospital with bulbs hanging from the ceiling assailing his vision. He was struggling to keep awake.

'Stay with me, Andy,' Lucy cried again and again while dragging dying Anderson to the operation room with three doctors.

Lucy was not allowed to enter the operation theatre and doctors shut the room once Anderson had been taken inside.

Anderson's whole life flashed before his eyes while he heard the doctors going on about technical medical terms that were absolute gibberish to Anderson's ears. The doctors had never seen such fatal wounds before and were thinking if the traditional way of operation could save him. In moments, doctors drugged Anderson to make him unconscious and began operating on the wounds. They had already given Anderson the antidote of the virus he had injected during the fight against Johnson as the last resort, and that had purged Anderson's system from the virus. The antidote had been given to the doctors by Lucy.

*

Anderson heard the chirping of birds and slowly he opened his eyes. The first thing he saw was his favourite person in his world. His girlfriend, Lucy, sitting on a chair near his hospital bed.

As soon as Lucy saw him sit up, she stood up immediately, her eyes with tears of happiness. Anderson observed his surrounding. He was hooked to three different types of machines. One thing he found weird was that he had some text flashing before his eyes as if he were staring at the screen of a computer terminal. The next thing he found was that was something odd about his hands which were under the cover of the bedsheet. He pulled them out and he couldn't believe what he was seeing. He had slick black metal where there should have been flesh and skin. The same was with the legs too. He had robot arms and legs. However, he observed that his upper body remained human. His eyes started flashing instructions.

'What have they done to me,' Anderson started to panic.

Lucy picked his hands and looked into his eyes. 'The doctors did all they could, but this was the only way to save you. They replaced your heart with an artificial one. Natural limbs were not compatible with the artificial heart so they had to replace your limbs too. There is a chip installed in your brain that will help control your limbs like you used to with natural ones.'

For a long moment, Anderson said nothing but stared at nothingness. 'What are these texts, numbers and instructions flashing before my eyes?' Anderson asked finally when he was over the grief of losing his humanity.

'It is your Hud, the heads-up-display, enhanced vision. You will see everything differently now. The doctors will help you understand the information displayed on your HUD,' Lucy explained.

'How long have I been out?' Anderson asked while scratching at his neck.

'It has been two weeks, Andy,' Lucy replied. 'And that's a jack for firmware maintenance of your brain chip at the back of the head. Don't mess with that,' Lucy warned. 'Through that socket, the doctors will keep the software on the chip up-to-date. Now, it's running the stable version 1.0.2 as per the doctors.'

'What happened at the night Johnson got into the building?' Anderson asked, the scenes of the battle against Johnson flashed before his eyes.

'Johnson killed all the securities and apprehended the boss,' Lucy replied.

'He is one tough son of a bitch, I give you that,' Anderson admitted.

Lucy continued, 'Lucian was then taken to the holding cell in the Federation's HQ and was kept there, but three days later he was moved to the Maximum security prison in Dimitry district. He has a death sentence on his head and they will electrocute him after making him serve the prison time for two years. Without him, the Lutsi will be no more. The bioweapon of Dr Serizawa has been captured by the Federation and they will use it to make the antidote for the virus.'

Lucy paused for a moment before continuing, 'The Federation's people have arrested all of the personnel working in the Flash building. I barely escaped with you.'

'How the hell you got me out of the building. I weight bloody eighty kilos?' Anderson asked in bewilderment.

'First, I cloaked us with Nanotech's GCR device, making us invisible, and then I drugged myself with the Injection of Strength of Hercules, acquiring temporary inhuman power to haul your limp body on my shoulder and to my car parked outside in the parking lot,' Lucy explained.

'Strength of Hercules, you say? Isn't it extremely dangerous for health? If not careful with the correct dose, you could have some serious heart disease with that later in your life,' said Anderson.

'It seemed the only way to me at that time. And don't worry. The doctors have examined me and told me that the drug has been absorbed by my system successfully and will be out of my body soon completely via urine,' Lucy said.

'Thank you, Lucy, for saving my life,' Anderson said with a mild tone.

'Andy...'

'Yes, Lucy...'

'I guess it's time we moved on and found a new life, you and me,' Lucy said after a moment's hesitation.

Anderson missed the hint there in Lucy's sentence and voice because his mind was shrouded by the anger at the defeat at the hands of Johnson. 'Maybe, I have last gas left in me for one final assignment. I want to rescue the boss and put a bullet into the heart of that Steven Johnson and leave him to die, just like he did to me,' Anderson said, the fire of revenge gleaming in his eyes.

'No, Andy. You need to let it go. No good has ever come from this cold dish called revenge. Who knows what might happen to you if you went on to do that? No, I won't let you walk on that path. It's a miracle that you have been saved and I'm not sure if there will be a second one. No, I don't want to lose you, Andy. I love you with all my heart and I'm not sure I can bear to live without you.' With that said, Lucy locked her eyes with those of Anderson and they stared at each other with passion for some time, until both ended up kissing each other wildly.

*

Two years had passed since the event of the apprehension of his boss of Lutsi, the terrorist organization, and one and a half years since Anderson and Lucy had got happily married. In ten days, his former boss, Lucian Lee would be electrocuted in the prison of Dimitri district after having served the two years of prison time. Well, that was not Anderson's problem now. He had moved on to a quiet new life with his wife Lucy and his two-month-old daughter Alexandra. During his teen time, Anderson had always shown a passion for the game of cricket and now he worked as a well-respected coach of that game. It was 8:00 PM and he was in his Maruti seventh-generation 7001 black car that he piloted in the air in airway number eighty-seven. That was much traffic today on eighty-seven and Anderson was forced to fly at a speed that was not more than forty-five km/h. It would still take him an hour to reach home and he was getting impatient. Of all the high numbers his fast car's speedometer's needle could point, it was stuck on forty-five.

'Move it, pal,' Anderson yelled after poking his head out of the car's window while honking the car's horn. But it had no effect on the traffic. He had no choice but to stick to airway number eighty-seven.

The ministry of airways had established certain lines in the air they called airways. Every driver who wanted to fly his vehicle in the air had to fly through one of these airways. Any flying outside those airways would be considered illegal and the driver breaking the rule would get a memo or jail time. Every now and then, floating drones kept the airway under watchful eyes. Anderson saw a patrolling traffic police car fly past him outside the airway number eighty-seven. The general rules didn't apply to traffic police. They could choose to fly their vehicles anywhere and anyhow they desired as long as they kept the citizens from breaking the traffic rules.

Every vehicle had to mandatorily install a special HUD gadget approved by the ministry of airways. The gadget would be attached to the corner of the car's windshield, completely out of sight, and would provide a heads-up-display covering the whole windshield showing the available airways in the air in the form of colourful lines and curves mimicking the actual roads on the land. At every kilometre, there was an airway called To-Land that led to the road on the land. The vehicle in front of Anderson used one of those To-Land airways to move down to the road beneath which was several feet below.

When he finally reached the proximity of the district where his home was, after blinking the car's signal, he left the busy airway eighty-seven and with the help of a To-Land airway, landed on the road on the ground. Once on the road, he switched the airborne mode off and the heads-up display automatically vanished from his car's windshield. It was now just fifteen minutes drive from that point to his home. It was a good life for Anderson. He had a good-paying job, a loving wife and a daughter. But good has a nasty habit of never lasting for long, which Anderson would find about tonight.

The road was flanked by an open landscape under the crescent moon, and in the distance, Anderson saw the city teeming with various lights. Above in the sky, the airway number eighty-seven looked like a line of fireflies stretching infinitely at both ends.

Anderson turned on the car's music system and put on some jazz music to relax his mind before accelerating the car. Slowly, the car's red taillights became smaller and fainter as the car headed to the city in the distance.

CHAPTER SIX

THE PRISON BREAK-OUT

Lucy was stirring the meal in the vessel, trying to cook something new for the dinner tonight. She checked the other vessel on the electric stove which contained milk for Alexandra, her daughter.

Once the milk had heated enough to kill all the bacteria in it, she poured it into the baby bottle for feeding her daughter. She once again stirred the meal on the gas stove and switched the cooling mode on of the baby bottle. Once the milk in it has become to room temperature, she switched the bottle's cooling mode off and carried the bottle to the bedroom where Alexandra slept in a cradle which was decorated with spinning toys.

No sooner had she fed Alexandra with milk than loud raps on the main door sounded. 'Dady's home, honey,' Lucy said smiling and in response to that Alexandra baby-chuckled. Lucy placed the bottle on a stool beside the cot, put the cot in an automatic swing at level two and exited Alexandra's room to answer the door.

Lucy placed his palm on the scanner of the door and the door unlocked. As soon as she opened the door she found that it was not his husband that stood there.

'Hey, Lucy. Long time no see,' the man in a long coat greeted.

'What are you doing here, Ralph. I no longer work for Lutsi,' Lucy said and tried to shut the door on the man's face. But the man called Ralph blocked the door with his hands.

'Don't be daft, Lucy. The boss never released you. You should've read the contract well while signing it. You're still an employee of Lucian Lee. You and that husband of yours,' Ralph said.

'I don't care what the contract says, we don't give a damn about Lutsi anymore. Go now before I call the cops,' Lucy warned.

Lucy was just about to reach for her cellphone in her frock's pocket to call the police when Ralph quickly brought his left palm up and from the mouth of the tube that ran along his arm, he gassed Lucy. As soon as the gas got into Lucy's system she fainted and fell with a thud to the floor.

*

Anderson parked his Maruti 7001 in the garage at bungalow number 34 and walked to the door. He rapped the door and waited. When Lucy didn't answer the door, he rummaged for a key in his pockets. After finding it, he unlocked a box attached beside the door and opened it, revealing a green panel. He unlocked the door by giving his palm's scan to the panel. He shut the panel's box and turned the key in it before entering the house.

'Honey, I'm home,' Anderson said as he said every evening when he got home. Usually, he would get a response from Lucy immediately either from the kitchen or from Alexandra's room. Upon not hearing her voice, he went to investigate. He checked all the room and the kitchen but he couldn't find Lucy or Alexandra.

Has she gone somewhere without telling him? He thought. But why would she leave the house at this time?

He tried to call her but her cellphone was coming switched off. He panicked and started to walk back and forth in the living room, trying to decide whether should he call the police or not.

When he was about to key in 911, a beeping sound came to his ears. He looked at the source of the sound, which was from a small cubic device lying on the surface of the round glass table, which in all his stress Anderson had missed to notice before. It was a hologram messaging bot.

He pressed a micro switch in it with the tip of a pen and the cube came to life. Small particles danced in the air and a 3D image was formed.

'Hey, Leo. Just in case you haven't noticed, we have got your wife and daughter. And don't worry about them. They are safe, for now. If you want them back alive, do as I say. In fifteen days the boss will serve the death sentence. Get the Lucian Lee out of Maximum Security prison. I have already set up a team of three capable men and you're the fourth one. See me in Norton's Junkyard tomorrow at midnight. I and the rest of the team will be waiting for you there. Do come alone or else say goodbye to your family.' With that, the particles that had formed the 3D image started to separate.

From inside, Anderson was boiling like hot lava with rage and he vented his anger by smashing the glass of the table with his fist and throwing the hologram projection cube at the wall with the insane force given by his prosthetic arm. Every inch of his mind was telling him to go gun blazing at the junkyard and kill all of the bastards. But that could jeopardize his family. He sat on the couch all night with his head buried in his hands, his mind going on a rollercoaster of emotions.

*

Anderson was walking among the tall piles of garbage in Norton's junkyard at midnight. The place was reeking and Anderson had to wrap a handkerchief around his neck to keep the smell from assailing his nostrils. At the heart of the junkyard, he found what he had been looking for, the kidnapper of his family - Ralph.

Ralph was with six well-armed men. And there were three differently attired men he talked with. As soon as Ralph spotted Anderson walking toward them, his all attention steadied on him.

'Well, hello there, Leo. I thought a man like you wouldn't change a bit, but, I see you have,' Ralph called while spotting his prosthetic limbs for the first time.

'Don't worry about that. With these robot parts, I'm now five times the badass I was before. Enough powerful to take you and your group of armed men out tonight,' Anderson said with confidence but then hesitated for a moment before replying, 'But, you have targetted at my weak point - my family. So, I won't do anything stupid. Tell me your scheme. I want to get it over with quickly and be my family once again. But first, let me have your words that Lucy and Alexandra are safe.'

'Oh, they are safe all right. My men are taking good care of them. Now, would you mind coming closer, I want to introduce you to the rest of your team,' Ralph instructed and one by one the three differently attired men were made acquainted with Anderson.

Once all men had become familiar with Anderson and vice versa, Ralph offered 3D pair of glasses to Anderson. 'Put them on and we will go over the plan.'

Anderson, Ralph and the three men on the team put the glasses on. Ralph then put a small cube, produced from his pocket, on the ground and all men surrounded it. There was a beeping sound from the cube and a 3D picture in the form of colourful lines and curves burst out of it for all the five men wearing special 3D glasses to observe. The plan was top secret so it required specially encrypted 3D glasses to see.

They all went over the plan three more times before packing it up and dispersing under the moonlit night. In a few minutes, the junkyard was empty again.

*

Lucian Lee was lying on his small bed in his dark cell of the maximum-security prison in Dimitri district when a deafening explosion took out a whole wall of his small cell. With the wall gone, the cell was flooded with sunlight. A man entered through the smoke and into the cell.

'It's me, boss, Leo, ' Anderson said.

Lucian looked puzzled.

'Your son, Ralph Lee has sent us to get you out.' Anderson said and after grabbing his right hand he led him outside the cell where three men of his team were giving covering fire with assault rifles. The claxon bleated madly all around the prison, suggesting a prison break-out is in progress. Billie, Cage, Mike and Anderson had used fake identities of cops and had entered the compound of the prison. The system couldn't detect them since Ralph had hacked and uploaded their fake identities to the police database system. It would still have taken a few more hours before those fake profiles were detected by an anti-cheat program.

All four armed men and Lucian were ducked behind a prisoner carrier truck, pinned down by five snipers from watchtowers protecting the main giant gate of the prison yard. Billie activated his body shield and pulled out a sniper rifle of his own. He took three sniper shots, which were absorbed by his energy shield while taking out all five of the snipers in watchtowers. More reinforcements came and all four men became busy defending against all of the cops that tried to stop them.

They didn't have to escape the prison yard according to the plan. They just needed to hold their positions while keeping Lucian Lee protected until Ralph brought in the Bird F13 - the latest and greatest in all of the hovering planes.

It had been fifteen minutes and Anderson had been pressing a red button non-stop to signal Ralph for evacuation. 'Where the hell that guy is at?' Anderson muttered to himself.

Then, like a flying angel, the big bad bird showed up to take Anderson and his team out of there. First, the bird got into hovering mode and fired a pair of machine guns, forcing all of the resistance to retreat. Then while giving cover fire, Anderson yelled at his men and Lucian to go for the bird.

Rope ladders were thrown down from the plane and each one of the men grabbed one. But then suddenly a tank entered the yard firing at the bird. To keep the plane light it only had machine guns and that was not enough to destroy the tank.

Anderson let go of the rope ladder. 'Go, all of you. I'll take care of that tank,' He yelled and fired a barrage of bullets at the tank to get its attention. But the tank was concentrated completely on the bird.

The rope ladders had pulled each man into the plane. 'We gotta go, The bird can't take it anymore,' Lucian yelled, over the cacophony of the plane's engine added with hundreds of guns and a heavy battle tank firing at the plane, at his son who was on the pilot's seat pushing all kinds of buttons and flicking various switches madly.

'But Leo is down there,' Ralph yelled back to his father over the loud noise.

Anderson knew that If anything happened to that plane, he would lose his family, so without any hesitation and thinking for himself, he ran towards the tank.

Anderson saw that the plane was leaving and the tank had its gun still set on it, firing shot after shot in the air. Anderson took that to his advantage and climbed on the top of the tank before opening the hatch and lobbing a frag grenade in it. He quickly shut the hatch down and jumped from it before the tank exploded like hell.

Anderson had been caught in the explosion but due to his prosthetic strong body, he didn't die there but instead lay on the ground groaning in pain a few meters from the destroyed tank in flames. He was lying on his back, in pain, while his vision slowly filled with faces looking at him in police uniforms. With the comforting knowledge that the plane had successfully escaped with Lucian Lee, and his Lucy and Alexandra would be free, he then started losing his consciousness.

*

The plane in which Lucian travelled switched to airship mode and headed towards a space station called Lambda in space. The auto-repair function of the ship had taken care of all the minor damage done by the tank at the prison. The space station they were heading toward was visible from the earth as a small dot during the daytime.

After three hours of ascending in space, the spaceship landed on a VIP docking bay. From there, Lucian, his son and the three men walked down the ramp and entered the spaceport. Since there was no air in the space, the whole station was shielded with a layer of energy to keep the artificially produced oxygen from leaving the atmosphere.

Outside the spaceport, a fancy black limousine waited for them which would drive them to their new Lutsi headquarters Ralph Lee had established in the absence of his father. Since the sun never shone on this space station, it was always a night despite the time showing 13:00.

The limousine passed a busy bazaar street followed by a highway. Fifteen minutes on the highway and they entered a town with tall buildings. The driver continued to drive the car until they reached a dingy looking old five-storey building. There was a garage and the driver parked the limousine in it.

'Welcome to the new headquarters, dad,' Ralph said to his father, smiling. 'We are on a kind of budget after our fall two years ago at the Flash building. But things are improving and our drug and weapon business is prospering here. Maybe soon we will have the luxury to have a Flash-like building once again for our headquarters. Anyways, Let's go inside and have a meal 'coz I'm starving. After we've eaten, I'll show you around your office. You will love it.'

Lucian Lee thought if his life would be any better than that in the prison where he had become institutionalized and had started to feel at home? Maybe not, but hey, he wouldn't have an electric chair waiting for him anymore.

*

Steven Johnson was in his apartment, seated on a couch in front of the TV, watching the news while eating from a bowl of noodles, when suddenly a news story that started to roll on the TV screen got his full attention.

'This is just in,' the lady anchor said. 'There has been a breach in Maximum security prison in Dimitri district and a prisoner named Lucian Lee, who ran a criminal organization formerly known as Lutsi, has escaped with the help of a group of men wearing false identities of police officers. One man was captured in the process and he is currently being held in the prison for interrogation. And now for the weather report, we will move to Kelly, but first words from our sponsors.'

Johnson switched the TV off and got dressed to go to the Dimitri district to meet this captured guy. The news hadn't shown any picture of him, so he had no idea who it was.

After locking his apartment door he entered the lift and reached the ground floor. He walked to his white Nisan T300 parked in the underground parking lot before entering his car and heading out for the Dimitri district.

*

Anderson hung from the ceiling, upside down, with a rope, in a dark room. With his inverted vision, he saw the door open. A man entered the room holding a baton. He then walked to a wall and flicked something that turned on a five-watt dim, hanging bulb from the room's ceiling. Anderson squinted in the sudden flooding of the light as his pupils had adjusted to the dark of the room before.

Anderson was half-awakened due to the extreme punishments he had been taking since he was captured. The man that had just entered the room had visited Anderson five more times before in this room. At each visit, he had beat the hell out of Anderson with his baton. Once done with his session of beating, he would turn the five-watt bulb off and leave the room and would return after half an hour to repeat. Anderson was not giving what they wanted, and that was the information on where their prisoner, Lucian Lee, had escaped to.

After fifteen minutes of beating helpless Anderson with his baton, the fat police officer reached the limit of exertion and was perspiring like a pig. Wiping the sweat off his brow, he switched the light off and left Anderson in the dark.

After an hour when the door reopened, the silhouette in the darkness of the room told Anderson that it was not that fat officer with the baton in his hand. When the light was turned on, even though with his inverted vision, he recognized the face immediately. It was Johnson, Steven Johnson.

'You...look familiar,' Johnson said. After a moment of rummaging through his memory, Johnson said, 'Wait...you're the guy that I battled with in the Flash building two years ago. I remember putting a bullet in your heart. How did you survive that?'

Anderson spoke nothing but stayed silent.

'I see you have a few prosthetic enhancements,' Johnson said when he spotted his robot arms and legs. 'Are they of Victor industries of America or Yang industries of China?'

Anderson didn't break his silence.

'Look, this prison is a hell hole. The food here is not good and the police officers here are rude and ruthless. I can make a transfer to the Federation's prison, which is a much better one compared to this. You would be able to serve your sentence there in peace. All I need to know is where Lucian Lee is now,' Johnson said in a friendly, mild tone.

When he heard no response, Johnson continued to persuade him, 'Look. I can get you what you want, just tell me where the escaped prisoner is.'

Finally, Johnson's friendly words got to him and Anderson said at last with tears, 'I want to be with my family again.'

'Where is your family? I'll give it a call,' Anderson said.

'I don't know where they are now. They were prisoners the last time I spoke to them.' Anderson said.

'Prisoners of who?' Johnson asked.

Anderson said nothing but shook his head.

'I can help you locate your family. Just let me know who they were prisoners of?' Johnson asked.

When Anderson heard the sincerity in the man's voice, he decided to rely on him for help, 'Ralph Lee, the son of Lucian Lee, had kidnapped them and was holding them hostage at Lambda space station. The only way I would be able to free my family was to join them in an operation of breaking Lucian Lee out of the prison.'

'Where Lucian was going to be taken at Lambada?' Johnson asked.

'I've not seen the place but they've given me the coordinates, which I could give you if you let me go,' Anderson proposed an offer.

Well, he is just a man with hands tied, doing what he was doing to save his endangered family, Johnson thought to himself. After a moment of thinking Johnson concluded, I could trade him for Lucian Lee, I suppose.

Johnson locked the room's door from inside and cut Anderson free. He then pulled a pistol from his pocket and pointed it at Anderson. 'If you ever thought of trying to betray my trust on this...' Johnson suddenly fired the gun, which he knew wasn't loaded and gave a sharp click, which was enough to make a point to Anderson. 'Now, tell me the coordinates.'

'Not, yet. First, get me out of this shithole.'

'Humm...One of those "you scratch my back I scratch yours" things, eh?' Johnson said and handed him the empty gun, which Anderson hesitantly accepted.

'Look, I have a plan,' Johnson said nodding at the pistol. 'You know it's empty, I know it's empty, but they don't know it's empty,' Johnson said mysteriously.

'What you wanna say?' Anderson asked.

'Ever tried a human shield before?' Johnson hinted at his plan and after a moment when Johnson's plan had dawned on him and when he had found that Johnson also knew to play the dirty game, an ear-to-ear smile crossed Anderson's face.

*

All of a sudden, the door of the room holding Anderson burst open and Anderson came out with Johnson in front as a human shield, a gun pointed at his temple. The police in the corridor quickly pulled their pistols and aimed at the two men.

'Drop your weapons, all of you or I blow the brains of this poor man,' Anderson yelled threateningly as if he were going to do it with an empty pistol somehow.

Officers obeyed and one by one put their guns on the floor.

'Now, put your hands on your head and stand next to the wall, facing it,' Anderson commanded.

Officers here were assholes and they didn't give a damn if an innocent's blood was spilt, but they feared the news channels tearing down their reputation and probably a job suspension for having killed an innocent in a confusion, so they did what they had been told.

Both men then crossed various parts of the prison, with Anderson telling the officers and staff to lay down on the floor and the ground. When they passed a long corridor of holding cells, the prisoner behind the bars rooted and cheered for Anderson with loud voices and making wild noises. Eventually, they exited the main, large prison door and broke into one of the parked cars outside, before hardwiring it and driving away in it.

CHAPTER SEVEN

THE LAMBDA SPACESTATION

'So, you two wanna work for us...' Ralph Lee looked into the legal papers of their identities 'Ken and Vladimir?'

'Yes, I do,' said both Ken and Vladimir at the same time.

'Jacob already told me how nicely you delivered to our customer the merchandise, that is a hundred kilos of the banned drug, Strength of Hercules. I am very impressed. No police or anyone got any slightest hint of your work,' Ralph admired.

'Does that mean we're hired?' Ken asked excitedly.

'Yes, but you'd be in tier one for now and would be paid accordingly. Want to increase your payroll, then perform well and move up to the next tier,' Ralph explained.

'Fair enough,' Vladimir answered.

'See Jacob in the garage, he will give you your next assignment,' Ralph said and waved both men out of his office.

Both men used stairs to reach the ground and entered the garage. The packets of white merchandise, more of the Strength of Hercules, were being loaded by a bunch of men in a van. One of them was Jacob.

'Yo daug, to whom I'm to deliver this white lady this time?' Ken asked in his funky voice, exited for his second mission.

Jacob walked to Ken and handed him a screwed piece of paper that bore the name of the customer as well as the delivery destination. Ken opened it and read the bad but legible handwriting before putting it into his denim jeans pocket.

Once the van was loaded with the merchandise, Ken and Vladimir drove the vehicle out of the garage and headed for the delivery destination.

*

Once the merchandise had been delivered to a customer called Joseph Smith, Ken and Vladimir started the return journey back to the Lutsi HQ.

'You're sure this trick is gonna work, Leo?' Ken asked.

'Yes, it will,' Vladimir replied with confidence.

Ken and Vladimir were none other than Steven Johnson and Leo Anderson wearing high-quality masks, making them look like entirely different people. They wanted to be hired by Lutsi so that they could have their own living quarter in the Lutsi HQ. Anderson gifted Lucy a watch on her last birthday, which did more than just tell the time. It had a powerful GPS chip installed in it which would tell Anderson the approximate location of where Lucy was. With the help of that location, he was confident that his wife and daughter were still held in that building. But he didn't know on which floor and in which room they were. Their plan was simple. Once Anderson had located his family and moved them out of the building, Johnson would call in the Federation and in a few hours the personnel of the Federation would surround the building.

Johnson had advised going for the backup right away without bothering to go through all that Ken and Vladimir disguise. But, Anderson had refused it because he had deemed it too dangerous for his family, which would be inside that building during that time of heat. He wanted his family out of the building and out of harm's way before the situation became any possible intense at the HQ.

For the next seven days, both men, under the assumed identities, did errands in the van, delivering the Strength of Hercules to various high profile customers. By the eighth day, they had had their private quarters on the third floor of the Lutsi HQ building. Now, it was time to put the last stage of the plan into action. So, he left his quarters and in a kind of ninja way began walking through the corridors silently in the dead of the night.

Anderson opened the app on his smartphone for tracking GPS installed in his wife's wristwatch. The signal was there in the panel but weak, suggesting that he was still far from Lucy. He decided to take the stairs to the fifth floor. Once on the fifth floor, the strength of the signal improved, confirming that this was the floor where Lucy and Alexandra were being held. One by one he passed the rooms in the corridor seeing the strength of the signal fluctuate. It was midnight so all the corridors were empty. But Anderson was still trying to be very careful.

At last, he stopped at a room in the corridor, where the signal was the strongest. He tried to open the room but it was locked. The door's lock looked traditional enough, so he pulled out a hairpin from his denim jeans pocket and inserted it.

The sweat was covering his forehead while he turned the pin around in the lock with the thought that somebody might spot him. After long three minutes, the pin clicked in the lock and the door unlocked. The door didn't creak upon opening it and Andeson closed the door behind him after entering the room. When he saw Lucy lying on the bed, asleep, with Alexandra beside her, his throat choked with the happiness of seeing them after so many days.

He tip-toed his way to the bed and removed the mask he had put on of some other man. He had to do it else Lucy wouldn't identify him as his husband and might make things difficult.

'Lucy, wake up,' Anderson said silently in her ears. The eyes opened and Lucy saw him in the dim footlight of the room. When she was going to cry out in excitement, Anderson put his palm on her mouth to tell her to stay silent, and to that Lucy nodded.

Lucy with little Alexandra in her arms was slowly and silently following Anderson close behind. Anderson had a pistol with a silencer at ready in case he bumped into someone at this late hour of the night. Due to the tight budget of Lutsi, luckily, there was no night sentry posted in or outside the building and all other men were asleep in their comfortable beds.

In ten minutes they had exited the building through the main door. Anderson walked them off to the delivery van and handed her the key for the engine. Anderson also handed her a map and some money and told her to get to the spaceport in the north and wait for him there, before he started walking back to the door of the building. Anderson didn't bother to put on the mask back because once it was removed, the mask was wasted and could not be worn again. He had to return to Johnson to tell him that he could now call for backup. He could text him on the phone but Lutsi had given them only one phone, which was especially monitored by Ralph's men and they had to share it amongst themselves. Their own phones had been taken away by Ralph and destroyed on the day they had joined.

After five minutes, Anderson was with Johnson. They had broken into the computer room and were hacking a terminal to send an email from his personnel Ultramail account to the Federation for backup. The terminal finally accepted a password that Johnson had hacked. Once the browser was in incognito mode, he logged onto Ultramail's website and started typing the recipient, subject and the body of the mail. It took him barely a minute with his familiarity with the keyboard to finish sending the email. Everything was going according to the plan, but suddenly something happened, something bad. The anti-theft system of the terminal identified an unauthorized usage of a terminal and sounded a loud alarm across all floors. Anderson cursed in five different languages and both men braced themselves for the hell to break loose.

*

It was noon and the cover of Johnson and Andeson had blown. They were pinned in the corridor of the third floor, behind a wall in a corner next to the computer room, firing at the Lutsi's mercenaries. Merchinaries returned fire and both men hid behind the wall to avoid the bullets. They had been pinned in that corner since that damnable computer program had tracked Johnson down and turned on the alarm.

The backup arrived an hour ago and the personnel of the Federation had surrounded the building. All Anderson and Johnson had to do was to get the hell out of the building alive. Some sixty to seventy Lutsi men were in the way, and all Johnson and Anderson had was a gloak-17 pistol each.

'Last year, I got installed two powerful augmentations which are called a titan shield and the Icarus dash,'

Anderson said. 'Once the titan shield is activated, my body will be surrounded by nano indestructible particles which will give me a titan armour, deflecting all of the bullets fired at it for a limited time, let's say for fifty seconds. That would be enough to run through these guys and reach the exit door of the building using the ultra running speed of Icarus dash. But I haven't activated two augmentations at the same time before. My energy core might get overheated and explode,' Anderson explained. 'Plus, I would have to execute it perfectly at the first time, because, with one use, its batteries would die and can only be recharged at the prosthetic clinic before those skills become available to use again.'

'But how's it gonna help me get out?' Johnson asked.

'Didn't you have a piggie ride while you were a kid?' Anderson hinted him his plan.

Johnson shook his head in disbelief and said, 'You can't be seriously thinking me doing that embarrassing thing.'

'That's the only way,' Anderson said.

After a few minutes, there was a blur in the corridor and on the stairs, and the wooden exit door was broken from its hinges as both Anderson and his piggy rider, Johnson crashed through it with the strength of the titan armour and the speed of Icarus's dash.

Both men reached for the sky in front of the hundreds of Federation commandos aiming at them.

'It's me, Admiral Steven Johnson,' he said by removing his mask.

The chief commando named Bill immediately identified his face and told his men to get the bloody aim of the guns off them.

Johnson and Anderson walked to Bill who stood behind the line of energy shields employed by the commandos to protect them from returning fire from the mercenaries hidden in the building. 'How many men are there, admiral?' asked Bill.

'Probably sixty to seventy including the escaped prisoner, the head of the Lutsi, Lucian Lee,' Johnson replied.

Bill nodded at that answer and stared at Anderson suspiciously before replying, 'You are that prosthetic guy. You used the admiral as a human shield to escape the maximum-security prison in Dimitri district. I read it in news.'

Johnson borrowed handcuffs and the key of it from Bill and arrested Anderson. 'Don't worry, I'll be taking him back to the Dimitri district on Earth,' Johnson said.

'Okay, sir. I leave it to you then,' Bill said. He then grabbed a speaker and started speaking into it. The speaker amplified his voice loud enough that all inside the Lutsi building could hear him say, 'Now, this is my last warning to you. Surrender yourself and come out with hands above your heads. It doesn't have to be messy. Let's keep it clean by not getting any casualties from either side.'

In response to that, there came a burst of fire from assault rifles from the building windows. After that, the firefight between four hundred Federation commandoes and seventy men of Lutsi began, which mathematically was an automatic defeat for Lutsi.

Leaving the firefight behind and after borrowing the car from Bill, Johnson rode away with handcuffed Anderson.

When they had reached the spaceport in the north, Johnson tossed the handcuff's key at Anderson, which Anderson caught with his amazing reflexes. 'The deal is a deal. You played your part now let me play mine,' Johnson said.

*

The moment Lucy saw Anderson walking towards the passenger's waiting area, she stood up from the bench and leaving little Alexandra sleeping, waited with open arms to embrace her husband with all her heart.

Both hugged for like a full minute before Anderson pushed her to arm's length. 'Missed me?' Anderson asked.

Lucy nodded with tearful eyes and they both kissed passionately.

Two hours had passed and Anderson and his family had booked tickets and were climbing the ramp of a spaceship ready to blast off. The warrant for Anderson was still out there on Earth so he can't go to his home on earth with his family. He had decided to find a new life somewhere far away, and that's why he was climbing a spaceship bound for an earth-like planet called Xeon T15, which is inhabited by mixed species, in the G5.3 galaxy.

Anderson and Lucy turned back on the ramp and stared for a brief moment, both thinking the same thing that they would never have to see or hear about Lutsi again.

*

Ralph Lee, Lucian Lee and a group of seven Lutsi mercenaries were walking the filthy and stinky waters of the sewer. They had used a secret passage from the basement of the Lutsi's building that led down into the sewer. They had escaped the firefight and were now on their way to the spaceport. They were gonna use their spaceship parked in the VIP dock to get out of this space station and to planet Jamal, where Lucian would meet his boss and discuss their fall on Earth and Lambda.

Lutsi was more than a criminal organization run by Lucian. It was a widespread problem across the universe. Lucian was just a pawn of a huge body of Lutsi. The emperor was what they called their boss, who ran Lutsi's main HQ on planet Jamal.

After taking out the Lutsi HQ on earth as well as on Lambda space station and helping a man to reunite with his family, It is just a matter of time before Steven Johnson is faced with a new mission.

9 798887 044644

Printed by Libri Plureos GmbH in Hamburg, Germany